THE STORY OF JUMPING MOUSE

A NATIVE AMERICAN FOLKTALE

retold by Amanda StJohn • illustrated by Durga Yael Bernhard

The Child's World

Distributed by The Child's World®
1980 Lookout Drive • Mankato, MN 56003-1705
800-599-READ • www.childsworld.com

Acknowledgments
The Child's World®: Mary Berendes, Publishing Director
The Design Lab: Kathleen Petelinsek, Design
Red Line Editorial: Editorial direction

Library of Congress Cataloging-in-Publication Data
StJohn, Amanda, 1982–
  The story of jumping mouse : a Native American folktale / by Amanda
StJohn ; illustrated by Durga Yael Bernhard.
      p. cm.
  ISBN 978-1-60973-140-3 (library reinforced : alk. paper)
  1. Indians of North America—Folklore. 2. Mice–Folklore. I. Bernhard,
Durga, ill. II. Title.
  E98.F6.S763 2012
  398.2097—dc23   2011010900

Printed in the United States of America in Mankato, Minnesota.
July 2011
PA02086

*ihtokwe. Api.* Come in. Sit down. An old woman like me has many stories to share. When you listen to elders tell stories, you remind us that we still have gifts to offer. Then we live long, healthy lives. *Ikosi*, that is how it is.

Once there was a little mouse who listened to many things. He listened to the river. He listened to his elder, the bison. Little Mouse had a good heart. For that he was greatly rewarded. *Ikosi.* . . .

Little Mouse lived with his family under an oak tree with cinnamon-colored leaves. The mice ate the acorns from the tree and never went hungry.

Now, Little Mouse was the youngest mouse in this family, and he was also the most curious. He never stopped asking questions! "What is this?" he would ask, pointing with his tail.

Fat Mouse, his big brother, would answer, "That's a mushroom," or "Ish! Rabbit droppings." In this way, Little Mouse learned about many things.

One afternoon, Little Mouse heard a strange sound in the distance. It sounded like a hundred mustang ponies galloping at once. "*Nistes*, brother," he said, "what is this sound I hear?"

It was a river. Little Mouse's heart soared as he watched ducklings float along. "I am going to swim across this river!" he declared and ran toward it.

"*Kaya!* Don't!" called Fat Mouse. "I want to go first."

Little Mouse was always patient with his brother. "Okay," he said. "You go first."

Fat Mouse hurried to the river—*whoops!* He tripped on a pebble near the river's bank. He tumbled into the water. *Splash!*

"I'm going home!" Fat Mouse pouted.

Little Mouse did not go home with his brother. "I will cross this river," he declared.

First, he tried to swim across, but his legs were too short.

Then, he tried to ride on a turtle's back, but it dove underwater.

"What else can I try?" he wondered. That's when he heard a *ribbit, ribbit*.

It was a frog. "I will name you Jumping Mouse," she said. "You will have the power to cross this river. Jump into the sky as high as you can, Jumping Mouse."

Little Mouse crouched low. "*Hese!*" he whispered. "Fly!"

With all of his might, Little Mouse jumped. The moment he was in the air, his back legs grew longer and he became Jumping Mouse.

"*Maandaa!* Amazing!" cried Jumping Mouse. "I see so many new things."

Jumping Mouse pointed to snow-capped rocks in the distance. "What are those?"

Frog answered, "Those are the sacred mountains."

Jumping Mouse's eyes glittered. "Then I am going to the sacred mountains. *Ikosi.*" At that, he swam across the river and hopped into the prairie like a little kangaroo.

Jumping Mouse settled on a brown boulder. He admired the mountains, which seemed larger than before. "What would it be like to live up there?"

"Eagles know the answer," said the boulder to Jumping Mouse.

"Are you speaking to me, Boulder?"

"I am not a boulder," said the voice. "I am the bison you are sitting on."

The bison told Jumping Mouse his story. "I have gone blind. Only the eye of a mouse will heal me. Surely, I will die."

Jumping Mouse didn't want the bison to die. "I am a mouse," he announced. "I will say a sacred word that my father taught me. Then my eye will heal you."

As Jumping Mouse said the sacred word, his eye flew away. It landed on the bison and healed him.

"Thank you!" said the bison. "You are good medicine. I shall take you to the sacred mountains."

Jumping Mouse burrowed inside the bison's shaggy hair to hide from the hungry eagles in the sky. There, he rode to the end of the prairie.

"Be well, sacred one," said the bison. He trotted away, enjoying all that he could see.

Jumping Mouse sat down in the grass. He didn't know what to do next, so he took a little nap. When he woke up, the grass asked, "Did you have a good nap?"

"Are you speaking to me, Grass?"

"I am not the grass," said the voice. "I am the wolf you are sitting on."

The wolf told Jumping Mouse his story. "I lost my sense of smell. I cannot hunt for food. Only the eye of a mouse will heal me. Oh, mouse. Surely I will die."

"*Unsica*. Poor wolf." Jumping Mouse frowned. "Even though it means I will be blind, I give you my eye so that you may be well again."

Jumping Mouse whispered the sacred word. His eye flew away and healed the wolf.

"Thank you!" said the wolf. "You are good medicine. I shall take you into the heart of the mountains."

Jumping Mouse hid in Wolf's fur and was carried away. He listened as Wolf told him many stories about the mountains. At last, Wolf stopped.

"Hello," said a voice. Jumping Mouse recognized that voice—it belonged to the magic frog from the river. "Come and talk with me," she said.

Wolf said goodbye. *Sniff-sniff-sniff.*
He searched for rabbit tracks near the
berry bushes.

"Frog," said Jumping Mouse, "I
gave away my eyes. What will become
of me now?"

"Jumping Mouse," said the frog, "you
respect your brother. You listen to your
elders and neighbors. You help everyone
you can. You have been good medicine.
Now, I will share good medicine with you."

"Medicine for me?" Jumping Mouse's
whiskers twitched. "Really?"

"*Tapwi,* really," said the frog. "Jump
into the sky and see what becomes
of you."

At that Jumping Mouse leapt into the sky. As he did, his front legs turned into wings. He grew a golden beak.

Whoosh! Jumping Mouse glided higher in the wind. His eyes healed, and he could see better than ever before. "*Awwwwk!*" he squawked with joy.

"You are not Jumping Mouse anymore," called the frog. "You are Eagle!"

Ikosi. That is how it is.

Canada

The Northern Plains

United States

Mexico

FOLKTALES

Jumping Mouse is a story told by Native Americans of the Northern Plains. For hundreds of years, storytellers have shared this folktale with people they love. They did not read the stories from books, though. Each and every storyteller memorized the story of *Jumping Mouse* and recited it, or said it aloud, by heart. In 1985, a Native American man named Hyemeyohsts Storm wrote down *The Story of Jumping Mouse* so that people all across the world could fall in love with it.

In folktales, magic happens all the time. A character in a folktale might fall off a cliff without being hurt. Jumping Mouse's eyes fly out of his head when he says a sacred word. The eyes heal the bison and the wolf. Then, the frog magically turns the mouse into a beautiful eagle with perfect vision.

One reason folktales include magic is to entertain you with a fun story. Another reason is that Native American storytellers want you to know that when it comes to dreams, anything is possible. Jumping Mouse's dreams came true with magic, but his own actions also played a part. He listened to his elders and he acted generously toward the bison and the wolf. For that, he was rewarded beyond his wildest dreams.

ABOUT THE ILLUSTRATOR

Durga Yael Bernhard is the illustrator of numerous children's books, with topics ranging from natural science to multicultural themes. She has a deep love of African culture, Eastern and Western religion, and the natural world, all of which are reflected in her art. Durga's experience mothering three children has also shaped some of her most notable works, including *A Ride on Mother's Back: A Day of Baby-Carrying Around the World*. Durga is most known for her innovative concept books such as *In the Fiddle Is a Song: A Lift-the-Flap Book of Hidden Potential* and *While You Are Sleeping: A Lift-the-Flap Book of Time Around the World*.